Naughty Nata

Naughty Nata

DONNA DEAL

Printed in the United States of America

ISBN 978-1-64133-684-0 (sc)
ISBN 979-8-89114-293-0 (hc)
ISBN 978-1-64133-685-7 (e)

Library of Congress Control Number: 2021925216

Drama | Travel | Action and Adventure

2026.04.20

MainSpring Books
5901 W. Century Blvd
Suite 750
Los Angeles, CA, US, 90045

www.mainspringbooks.com

Table of Contents

CHAPTER 1

It's All A Game

IT WAS FALL OF the year and time for the regular golf group made up of our husbands, significant others, fiancés, fathers, brothers, sons and who really knows your grandfather could be in there too, to go on their one week trip to Myrtle Beach, South Carolina, The Golf Capital of the World! The most exciting place for golfing in the sun during the day and heading for the strip bars at night. That's right ladies, a man's away from home real fantasy entertainment that's going to happen regardless of how you feel about having a half-naked woman crawling all over him in front of his macho group of guys who sit and watch while their own penises are ready to jump out and grab that ass too! Oh, and if you think they don't touch your man's private parts, you better think twice. There's always one or two Naughty Nata's out there ready to get down and dirty. The majority of men in our lives choose to think there is absolutely nothing wrong with a little so call non sex all up in the thee, hands in their pants and tongue entertainment. Have they forgotten what foreplay is when it comes to having sex?

They say what you don't know won't hurt you, but what you are about to find out can just: devastate your relationship or maybe if you really don't care, a threesome might be your cup of tea! You might even think it's their privacy if they choose to be entertained in this way and believe me some of them get really private all right, in a box like room with plush velvet chairs, aromas that fill the room and plenty of exotic oils to arouse your man. Sometimes even with more than one stripper. Women of all nationalities and backgrounds with personalities of pussy cats ready to devour your man. After all you can't blame the Naughty Natas', it's how they make their living! You see these young Chinese and Russian girls are being trained, at an early age to go to America and bring back into their country as much money from our men and women as they can make. That's why these strip clubs love to hire them. They are obviously good at what they do to attract your man to them. The clubs get what they want out of your pockets and so do the strippers! They even risk prostitution because they know that money talks and they will get out of it. Hell, the Attorneys and Judges are even obsessed with this type of entertainment. Diplomats and Politicians are among the audience of these clubs. If you ever ride by some of the many, many strip clubs at the beaches you will see lots of vehicles with government and diplomatic tags.

CHAPTER 2

Secrets You Find In Laundry

Too THOSE OF YOU who think your man comes home to you with intentions of making love because he missed you so much and ready to perform the greatest sexual experience you ever encountered, think again! You just might be fooled sweetie! Check the laundry! Some men are destined to think with their penis first and use what's left of their brains last when it comes to playing around.

They come home with all their laundry ready to be washed. Gathering it up and heading for the laundry room can be the biggest mistake of a man's life. Hell, most of us have to beg, borrow and steal to get him to take his clothes to the washing machine, why do they bother now! Next thing you know you go to help with the laundry and he says he will do it. There's your sign and you don't need a comedian to tell you that! So you say to him, no honey I will be happy to do your clothes as I usually do anyway. No big deal right? Wrong! He hurriedly heads off to work not really paying attention to what you are doing. Kisses you good bye and you tell him to have a great day and your glad he's home. Separating the whites from the dark clothes are usually the first most women do. This particular morning there is not enough soap powder to do all the wash so you decide to do the white clothes first. You pick up a few pieces and all of a sudden, you, having a great sense of smell, there's a shirt in your hand with makeup and an exotic aroma that you can't quite get a handle on. Oh My God! He's been with another woman and your mind starts triggering thoughts that are just about to make you blow up. Trying to process all of this and fearing what you had hope would never happen in your marriage you ask yourself, did he have an affair? Was there another woman he took with him on his trip? Believe me everything runs through your mind. Have you watched too many soap operas where men come home with lipstick on their collars? You are in a panic and your mind just keeps playing devils avocet with you. You stew about it all day and feel like your brain is going to explode and your heart just races and your restless about when he's going to get home from work. Why? Because you just want to throw the article of clothing at him and scream at him but you don't exactly take that approach. You've had time to work this out a little in your mind and decide to give <u>him</u> the benefit of the doubt. You ask him if he was around any women while he was gone, maybe at a bar dand possibly danced with someone just being social or was there a wife of one of the golfers along that maybe hugged him when he met her. After all not all men leave their wives at home, some go along to shop until they drop, spend money, relax away from the kids and call it a good time!

Then reality sets in and you wait for answers to your questions and they are No, No, No until you pick up the article of clothing and ask why there is a perfume smell and makeup on his shirt. Then the look on their face changes so quickly, you can feel the heat coming from his face as he looks down and says, "We went to the titty bar"! You begin to feel the steam building up because now you know he was involved in some form of activity with another woman! So you say, "Did you have a lap dance"? suspiciously knowing damn well that he's going to have to say the word you really don't want to hear. "Yes", he says and you immediately turn on that I'm going to kill you mode. "Why is this makeup up here around your collar and at the bottom of the front of your shirt?" "Did she give you a blow job"? He replies quickly, "No", they aren't allowed to do that! Then, besides being so mad, you start to swell up and the tears start streaming down your cheeks. He looks at you and says "I didn't do anything wrong, it's just entertainment". You tell him you feel betrayed and that he cheated on you. After all another woman's half naked body was all over your husband to perform a hands on experience you never dreamed he would have with anyone else but you!

You thank him for having no respect for you and that your heart is broken and you go to a place in the house to let your emotions out and cry yourself to sleep. This is not a dramatic situation, it's very real and a devastating one for you to swallow for some of us women. For days, you ponder over it, not washing the shirt. You keep going back and forth picking it up and smelling it and wondering what she looked like, was she doing her lap dance in front of his friends or did she do it in that "private" room. It's just killing you inside because you are taking this to be as bad as if you caught him in a sexual act. Everything starts to come to mind and you go from that emotional feeling to the more revengeful thoughts of how to get even. Believe me when it comes to men, they can be so damned stupid. After all a man's brain is in his Penis!

CHAPTER 3

Guilty Pleasure

S EVERAL DAYS GO BY, you aren't really communicating other than through text messaging and even that is not going good. You hate the damn cell phone because all the two are doing is skirting around the entire situation and not communicating face to face. One night you're cooking dinner and your man comes home cornering you in the kitchen, touching your ass and kissing you on the neck and trying to arouse you to the point you will give in to him and head for the bedroom. Not! You're still very upset and disturbed what he did that you just can't fall for his thinking that all he has to do is get you in the bed and have passionate, crazy, sex with you. Notice I said sex not love, because he can't possibly love you to want to seek out sexual entertainment from another woman!

This type of behavior goes on for a couple more evenings and you are really beginning to wonder if there is more to his guilt feelings and he's hoping to turn you into a Naughty Nata.

Finally, one evening you go to bed early, you just want to close your eyes and try to get some sleep. After all, you've been awake for nights, with restlessness over all this bull shit. Your man comes sneaking quietly under the covers and starts rubbing you, shockingly on your back and you feel his large hands slowly caressing your body as he reaches for your hand and places it on his very hard penis. It's going through your mind you want him to make love to you but can you keep from doing it because you still feel that he needs some form of punishment or you just aren't sure if you can ever forgive him.

After all you still don't know how far his lap dance went with that stripper! In the meantime, he reaches into his bedside night stand for the two vials of oil that is made to make your sexual encounter even warmer. He slips the bottle into your hand and proceeds to help you with it. It's now getting "hot in here" and he's whispering in your ear that he wants you, loves you and needs you. All the words that a married man can possibly say when they know they've been caught at doing something wrong. Yes, he really does want you and in such a convincing way that your weakness bell starts ringing in your head, your mind is shutting down to everything that has happened over the past few days and you fall into his trap of making love and believe me when it's over your telling yourself how wonderful it was, that it couldn't have been any better!

Thoughts are dangling in your mind now that maybe Naughty Nata did you a favor after all because this was the best sex you had in months!

Now the real explosion for the evening comes when he tells you how sorry he is and hopes I will forgive him. Your thinking, you stupid fuck head, you just made love to me and you want to ruin it now by bringing up the whole lap dance event! Was that an intelligent move on his part or act of being guilty, you make the call!

The next day after he leaves for work, you say to yourself, what a dumb ass you are for letting him think he just got away with it and that everything is good between us now. Oh well, that's what you want him to think, right? Not everyone is going to think like you do, especially those who just don't care what their man does and has the mindset that he comes home to YOU! They are wondering why you are taking things this far. You're still thinking about how to justify it all and you are ready to start this journey of proof of just how far your man really would go in your absence. It's all to prove a point my friends and this can only get more interesting as this journey begins! Not only are you ready to find out why men frequent strip bars, but you are wondering why they are so stupidly spending their hard earned money on these women when, in most cases, they have everything they need right at home. Believe me what you would do for him in the bedroom should be all he needs to satisfy his lust for sex!

CHAPTER 4

Do It Yourself
Research Investigation

IT'S TIME TO PLAN a trip with the girl's for a weekend away to the beach for some fun in the sun only you aren't taking a bag, ball and a club with you. This trip you will never forget nor will your friends. You are about to prove to yourself and others why these men of ours can't resist the desire to have some other woman's boobies bouncing in their faces. The airport taxi was on its way to pick us all up. Our flight leaves at 4:00 pm and arrives at 6:15 pm.

We are checking into a luxury hotel in this downtown resort in another state. You are glad you have been able to get away and have some fun but you know in your heart that this is more of an investigating trip to find out what makes your man and a stripper tick. Changing into some of the wildest, sexiest outfits you have ever seen which includes see through low hanging tops, short leather mini -skirts with lace stockings of different patterns and colors, garters showing, and high heeled boots up and over your knees. Oh and don't forget you are wearing those favorite red thongs he got you to wear on your honeymoon. Believe me we were dressed for success! Giggling to yourself how ridiculous you feel because most of us are just plain everyday housewives who don't know the first thing about going to a strip club, especially to a man's club that allows women to attend. Calling for the limo to pick us up sharply at 9:00 pm we are ready to hit the most extravagant strip club on the strip itself that overlooks the entire city. As we pull up to the hottest one in town, which we are going to call "Pussy Cats Galore", just to save face and protect the innocent kittens that are about to enter, we exit the limo in style, laughing our asses off that we even dare to enter! Some of us are even having second thoughts!

Being the first in the door, you walk in and immediately notice the women on the stripper poles and dancing in the cages topless. No one pays attention to this daring group of women entering for the first time of their lives into a man's world of almost all naked women dancing. We noticed right away that men and women were putting dollar bills in the thongs of these dancers. We were approached by a topless waitress whom asked if we would like to be seated at a table near the dance floor and at first we hesitated but then we decided, hell yes, we are here to go all the way with this investigation. The two shyest girls in our group, Tina and Jan are about to turn around and leave when I grabbed Jan and said we made a promise to each other we would all go through this together, now is not the time to back away! Tina is shy but sometimes we all think there is something secretly suspicious about her. The waitress, not knowing what we were up too, kindly seated us right next to a perfect group of what appeared to be golfers. Almost immediately, before we even ordered our drinks, we were approached by strippers asking us if we were here for the experience of a lifetime. Smirking, I spoke up and said yes, do you offer lap dances to female customers? "Oh, Yes", they replied, we offer you the same services that our male customers are given. Here is our menu of many different services we offer publicly and privately. One of the other girls speaks up and says, "What possible private services can you offer us that's going to arouse us like you do our men when they come in here"? Right off the bat, we are told they don't discriminate against anyone's sexual experiences regardless of gender. Your money is as good to us as would be any male who walks through that door and frankly more women experience lap dances then men do these days! You ladies seem to be dressed for the occasion and you will find it a great place to pick up men tonight and married ones at that. We have a special back door price for you to sit in on watching how men react to us when we go beyond their needs for lap dances. Then the brave red head in the group of us speaks up and says, "so that's when you take them back and give them blow jobs"? "Oh, no "says one of the strippers named Nata , "We call that snorkeling here. That's not illegal"! With that we all burst out laughing. After revealing that this was the first time we all had ever experienced setting foot in one of these clubs, the strippers knew they were going to show us a good time and completely blow our minds.

The group of men of we were seated beside could not take their eyes off the strippers until intermission at which time they decided to order a round of drinks for our table. Right then I started thinking to myself, it really isn't just the strippers they go for but to pick up a woman for a one night stand as well. Three of the five guys wore rings on their fingers but that didn't stop them from trying to pick us up. We thanked them for the round of drinks and just expressed that we were here for the experience of what a strippers' life is all about. One of the men calls over a stripper and introduces her to us as Naughty Nata. He says she's the best waitress, best stripper and the best snorkeler in this club. Then the men all burst into a howling laugh! Her reputation bring men from all over the country he said. I can't wait to get here on our golf trip twice a year just to be with her. Men have been known to fight over her! Our stomachs are starting to become a little nauseous now knowing that he could very easily be one of our husbands and he's sitting here telling us his firsthand experience with this bitch! She really has the nerve but then again, like we've said to ourselves before, you can't blame her. This is how she survives and makes an extremely good living at it too!

This group of guys continue to tell their stories to us about these strippers and seem to be familiar with all them. You're now proving to yourself that this is how men carry on in the absence of their wives or girlfriends. After all, we were dressed for attraction and that was what we were getting from this group. Our plan is working!

CHAPTER 5

Strippers Tell All

IT WASN'T UNTIL AROUND 2:00 A.M that this club is hopping and I mean literally! As the morning moves forward we are just flabbergasted at what we are about to hear from several of the strippers who seem to have taken a liking to us. Not sure really why they started volunteering speaking to us except we've already blown a bunch of money in this strip parlor. The big bosom red head in our group decides she is going to be the first to ask for a lap dance but first she gets the stripper to agree to talk to her and tell her about herself while she is performing her service and the girl agrees to whatever she request. We will call our redhead, Judy and the strippers' stage name is Mayla. As Judy sits with drink in hand and a smirk on her face and eyes about to pop, she feels the heat of the night as Mayla starts dancing around her like a flash of lightning and moving her hips in a motion that is not only catching all our eyes but the attention of our male groupies next to us! You see what we are about to find out is that the men in the group love watching a woman receive a lap dance more than they like watching other men having one. Judy proceeds to start asking Mayla what makes her tick as a stripper, why she picked this profession and if she ever thought what it might do to some man's wife or girlfriend if they found out. Mayla just laughs and replies "It's a job I make excellent money stripping and dancing. I am a single Mom with two small children that get hungry and need clothes on their back and a roof over their heads!" With that she moves forward with her tits right in Judy's face, her hands just stroking each one as if she's trying to put her nipples close to Judy's mouth. The expression on Judy's face was like any minute she was going to knock this chick off her lap. Mayla tells Judy she's trained not to pay attention to their reactions but to perform, get paid and move on to the next one. "Occasionally" she says , "you run across men that want more from you outside the club and will pay you to meet them at their hotel room when you get off work and even though that is considered to be prostitution and is illegal you do it anyway because the money is too damn good to turn it down." At this point we are all thinking to ourselves these strippers would rather take the chances of getting caught to make money on the side.

As the night goes on Judy decides she's had enough and tells Mayla that she thinks what she does for a living is terrific even though she is thinking to herself that she could wrap her hands around her neck and choke her to death. Mayla actually ask her if she and her friends would like to be entertained in the private room. "What kind of private room"? Judy asked. Mayla replies, " Oh, let me surprise you ladies because I have the expertise of knowing that your group would like more excitement for the evening". Judy says "Yes" before any of us have a chance to even think twice about it. OMG! I'm about to explode because I think maybe we are taking this a little too far. Needless to say, Mayla very nicely escorts us back to the VIP room! Hey we earned it didn't we to brave such an experience!

CHAPTER 6

The VIP Room

AS WE APPROACH THIS room we notice dark tinted glass with candle light flickering that just made it look very sensual. Mayla speaks very softly telling us to have a seat anywhere we desire in the room and ask if we would like to order a bottle of champagne. Of course, by this time we are already on our way to being blitzed, what's one or two more going to do. I decided to play the role and go along as the next one to take this to the next level. I very quickly asked what the towels and oils were for and why is there a chocolate fountain. I made everyone's faces flush more than they already were because I was heading in a direction of I'm up for anything to happen. And believe me it did. I have to tell you Mayla was very good at what she does but when Naughty Nata entered the room we all knew we were in trouble. She caught my eye first and reached out to me to stand up and come closer to the chocolate fountain. As

I turned around there were two other strippers bringing in huge strawberries and placing them on a beautiful glass mirror table in front of the other girls. I could feel the heat from the fountain and about that time Nata puts a bowl under it to catch some warm and very sweet smelling chocolate in it. In her other hand she is holding some satin material that seemed strange to me and it actually turns out to be a red satin robe in which she throws over top of a stand up wicker room divider and asks me to go behind and take off whatever I want to and at the same time saying the more I take off the more exciting it's going to feel for me. As I walked out with this gorgeous sexy feeling robe so short that my garters were showing I was asked to disrobe and lie down on this table covered with soft velvet pillows and sheets. The other girls are gasping for air but not saying anything and they to be in some kind of trance. I was beginning to wonder what was in the champagne we drank because I was feeling like I was having an outer body experience. I seemed to just fall right into the motions of what was happening as if I was in a fantasy world.

Then it just happens, I felt this warm chocolate being poured all over my body and the smell was so sweet and taunting that all I wanted to do was just dip a strawberry in it. As I took a quick look at the other girls before things started happening, I could see they were being served with strawberries, chocolate and whip cream. It was like they were being distracted from me and they seemed to be distorted just a little. What was going on I thought, I feel drugged? I could hear voices but I wasn't able to determine who they belonged too. All I really knew was that Nata was massaging my body with one hand and feeding me strawberries dipped in chocolate with the other. Mayla was on the other side with her hands rubbing my breast and never even thought about stopping her for one minute. Don't stop I thought and then I started to feel other hands on me and seemed like Nata had put down the strawberries and she proceeded to use some kind of vibrator running it down my belly and over parts of my body in a teasing like motion and I'm just so relaxed that I really don't care what happens next. She asked me if I ever had used a massage vibrator and I told her I hadn't. She slipped it into my hand and it felt like had a real penis shaped object in my hand. I couldn't believe what she told me I could do with it next if that was my desire. I turned my head and opened my eyes I saw that my friends were no longer in the same spot in the room but in a Jacuzzi shaped like a champagne glass and they seemed to be completely naked and laughing. I knew they weren't paying a bit of attention to me because they were squirting whip cream all over themselves. Nata softly spoke bringing my attention back to what she had just put in my hand telling me to imagine myself with my husband and fulfilling his fantasy of watching me perform with this object and enjoying the feel of the vibration. Before I knew it I was caught up into it and enjoying every minute of it. Twenty minutes later I was woken up by the other girls and wondering what the hell just happened. They were fully dressed and laughing their asses off because we were all caught up into a fantasy that we truly don't know how it started and ended. There was no red silk robe and no warm chocolate on my body and I was completely dressed. The smell of chocolate and strawberries was no longer in the room, the fountain was gone, the champagne Jacuzzi was no longer there, the strippers were all gone and Nata had disappeared. What happened to me is still today something

I will never figure out but I can tell you I never was aroused like that in my life. What all of us could say was that night was the experience of a lifetime!

CHAPTER 7

Behind the Tinted Glass

L EAVING THE VIP ROOM I noticed the tinted windows were no longer tinted and the room just seemed to have a secrecy about it now. We all started making remarks about the changes in the room and wondered if what just happened to us was for real. Looking at each other in awe and feeling very wired we headed back to the bar for more refreshments!

To our surprise the group of golfers that had been seated at the table beside us early on were no longer there and remember how they were the ones who introduced us to Nata, the best stripper around! Suddenly, within minutes of our conversation about them, we saw them coming out of the VIP section, down the hall and straight for the bar. It wasn't until they approached us and started trying to pick us up that I started to question how far the excitement we just experienced had gone.

They asked us to join them at their table and wouldn't take no for an answer. The ring leader for the group introduced himself to us as Toby. He kept staring at me as if he was undressing me, making me feel very uncomfortable and before I knew it we are all sitting at a table with drinks in hand enjoying ourselves. Toby speaks up to tell us what wonderful entertainers we were tonight and was glad that he hooked us up with Nata. Judy, the redhead, just about choked and spit her drink all over everyone. "What the hell are you talking about?" she said. Toby replied, "You know in the VIP room"! I spoke up and said," sure we went to the VIP room, but we saw all of you coming from that area too. What's up with the comments"? I was beginning to get very nervous and the rest of the girls were ready to call the limo to go back to the hotel, when Toby says "ladies, you had to know you were being watched through those beautiful tinted glass mirrors. Now come on he says, give me a break!" As hot as you gals looked when you walked through the door tonight, we knew there would be a good showing event! That's right, we paid Nata to perform with you ladies and she did exactly with you what we came here to see. "So the feeling of having been drugged. Was that in the game plan too?", I replied. Toby replies by saying "that was just a little extra boost you might say that was added to your champagne", "Not a bad play on our part, don't you think?" With that I raised my hand and slapped the living hell out of this guy and told him he should be put in jail for what he did to us. The rest of the guys just laughed it off and the youngest one in the group, Jake, says, "Anytime you ladies want to see your video we'd be glad to watch it with you". OMG! Judy kicked him in his nuts and the fight was on. The other girls headed for the door but Judy and I just couldn't leave it alone, we had to show these assholes what happens when you cross a redneck woman. Judy was on fire and I mean she lit into Jake while I was beating Toby over the head with a beer bottle. Here I am in the middle of a bar fighting like a man and all I was there for to begin with was research on what makes a man want a stripper and to find out how far they go with one. Well I found out alright.

They are cold hearted, conniving, sadistic mother fuckers who didn't deserve any woman much less be married to one.

It wasn't long before we heard sirens and the cops were headed in our direction. We decided it was time to leave this place and in a big hurry. Jan and Tina were already in the limo waiting for us at the front door. Needless to say, we got the hell out of there and headed straight to the hotel. We didn't want to talk anymore about it and we all felt like we had been run over by a mac truck. What a night!

CHAPTER 8

The Next Day

I T BECOMES APPARENT AFTER waking up the next morning and looking in the mirror, that none of us wanted to face daylight too quickly. Tina and Jan were both basket cases because of the news broadcast on the local TV channel or at least Jan was really emotional. Tina seemed a little subdued and told us to be quiet and listen. The police were looking for four women who may have been involved in an early morning strip bar brawl. They went on to say that these women were last seen leaving the bar in a white limo. Police are checking all leads into this matter and are seeking the help of the public to find these women. Also, one of the strippers that's associated with the strip club is wanted for prostitution, drugs, solicitation of porn and producing hundreds of videos without the permission of persons involved. It's suspected that the four men who were arrested last evening for destruction of property are involved in a sex ring with a local known stripper, Nataliya Votia, stage name Naughty Nata.

Judy and I are both about to throw up because as the news report gets more into detail of the brawl in local strip club, they reveal the condition of one of the men involved in the brawl was seriously hurt when he was hit over the head with a beer bottle by one of the women also involved in that fight. Another man was treated and released from the hospital and will survive his injuries. Judy speaks up and says "the bastards deserved what they got and we don't need to turn ourselves in because we've done nothing wrong. We were just protecting our rights"!

The news continues to report that Police are now checking all Limo companies who may have been hired by these four women. With that release of information, we looked at each other and basically said at the same time that we need to get the hell out of here as fast as we can and not turn ourselves into the police. Jan is ready to call her husband to come and get them. Judy and I convince her that we are in another state and no one knows who we really our because I planned this trip completely as an undercover type situation since we didn't want our husbands to find out. Our real names were not revealed at any time and we used a prepaid cash card for paying all our expenses. We used fake ID's arranged by Tina for us through her out of the country connection. Even the prepaid cash card was under my factitious name.

We now have no time to waste and we decided that we would split up in our travel back to our home state. I recommended that Judy go with Jan and I would go with Tina. Since our hotel was paid for, we just needed to leave through the side entrance. The local bus picked up at the hotel every fifteen or twenty minutes so we figured the police would be checking the airport since they had no idea how we arrived in this city. We all decided to take different buses in our chosen partner groups of two and head to the mall to get some disguises since the police already knew what we looked like from the surveillance cameras outside the strip club and who knows what other cameras were on us. Each one of us will become a different person by traveling as, Judy an older woman with gray hair, Jan a very shy and quiet younger woman with long hair tied in ribbons and bows, Tina a gothic female with fake tattoos and lots of chains and bracelets and last but not least there's me as a cowgirl with boots, hat, and tight blue jeans.

Our cell phones were prepaid so the communications between us would have to be minimal until we reached our halfway point which would be a four hour drive in the rental cars we picked up at the rent-a-car kiosk in the mall. We are now headed North in hopes of not being discovered by any law enforcement or anyone else for that matter. It was beginning to bother me that Nata disappeared so quickly without a trace as if she already had an escape plan in place. Were we somehow set up or did we get caught up in a ring of sexual maniacs!

CHAPTER 9

Halfway Point

WE ARRANGED BY CELL phones to meet at a Mom and Pop type restaurant so we wouldn't be around a large group of people waiting in lines at a big commercial restaurant. By the time we reached our designated spot we were all clinging to the fact that the news was steady broadcasting an alert to be on the lookout for us. Hell, we even saw the big Alert sign on the interstate crossing over the state line and I always thought that was meant to be for Amber Alerts only! Tina decides she is going to get on her cell phone and when I asked her what she was doing she said she had to leave a message for someone and wouldn't tell me who. I grabbed her cell phone away from her and told her she couldn't text anyone and questioned her acting so damn strange. It was as if she were preoccupied. Come to find out when we met up with Judy and Jan, Jan was upset because

Judy had thrown her cell phone out the window because she was trying to text her husband.

As we sat down attempting to get a good meal in us, you could see the stress just starting to come out of us. We all ordered beer because it was the only way to get relaxed. I even pulled out some anxiety pills and told everyone to take one because things were not getting any easier from this point on. The radio in the dive we were in was blaring out the same thing we had heard all the way up the road. All of a sudden, I just about swallowed my tongue when the announcer said that the man injured in the strip bar brawl was in a coma and not expected to survive his injuries. Judy looks at me and says, " Damn, Annette, I didn't know you hit him that hard!". I was totally freaking out and wondering what the next move should be with this situation worsening by the minute. Here we are wishing someone would say something and up pops Tina with a remark so shocking, coming from her, we all looked at her with disbelief! She said it was time for us to turn one of the cars in and all stick together as a group. She sure was coming out of her shell! The next thing out of her mouth was for us to continue investigating this problem and stay tuned to any news broadcast and the local newspaper. Her idea was to call our husbands and tell them that we were having so much fun that we want to stay a few more days. This would give some more time to plan the rest of our trip home without getting caught. She was starting to analyze and be more rational now which is good for Jan who was showing signs of getting her emotions on set. This meeting at the half way point is the best thing for all of us and we made a pack that we would stick together like glue and change our strategy.

Somehow over the next day we all became so attached to each other's hips. We stayed the night at dump motel just down the street from that dive we spent most of the day in and we were starting to feel the pressure like fugitives running from the law. We also were starting to let our disguises slowly slip away from us and becoming who we use to be. Not a very smart thing to do on our part but we were too busy trying to figure out how we could get to Jake, the youngest smart ass of that group of golfers they called themselves. After all he was the one who told us about the video that was made of us.

Here we are thinking that we only had so much time to check up on the guy named Toby who was in a coma in the hospital. We soon realized that we would have to leave this God forsaken halfway point, go back to where all this shit got started and regroup about how to find the missing video. Did Nata actually get away with it or did Jake have it. Who's to say that Toby didn't put it somewhere before the big brawl that night and now he may never wake up for us to find out. Art was a strange, kind of sneaky looking guy and he liked guzzling his beer one right after the other. You could tell he had an unhappy marriage by the way he talked about his wife. Although we never got introduced to the fifth man in the group, we seemed not to care because he looked and acted like a member of the Mofia with a foreign accent.

We only had a very slim chance of going back to the area where all of this took place without being caught, but Tina convinced all of us we couldn't return home to our families until we had that video destroyed. After all we really didn't know exactly what kinds of sexual acts we had participated in when we were entertaining those damn men. What we did know is we were under the influence of some kind of drug.

CHAPTER 10

Heading for Disaster

CLIMBING INTO THIS OLDER model silver Tahoe, we headed back down the interstate as if we feared nothing! Judy was fired up and wanted to go directly back to "Pussy Cats Galore", the strip club where it all got out of hand. Jan and Tina said they wanted to skin that little Jake alive and wanted to find out what Art's involvement was in all of this. We had stopped at a convenience store to get some gas right off the interstate and picked up a newspaper. First thing we find out is that all the guys except Toby were out on bail and Toby's condition was still the same and he was still in the hospital. This means to us that these guys are still possibly hanging out near the hospital so they could stay close to Toby. We were really just grasping at straws now, not knowing if these assholes had skipped town or not. Judy just reminded all of us that this group of guys seemed to be very close from the beginning.

Drinking coffee and munching on donuts we knew we had to get moving down the road and start making this plan come together. I decided that I would drive straight through for two more hours and we would arrive somewhere in the vicinity of the hospital and settle in for the night at one of the bed and breakfast homes near the hospital. There's no way that the cops would think we would be dumb enough to come back in the area so we played it cool for the next four to six hours after we arrived. Tina was the perfect one in the bunch to get her foot in the door as a nurse to find out for us what floor and room number Toby was on, but wait she didn't even know his last name. Tina had a plan and it worked perfectly. She walked up to a nurse's station on the first floor which was for critically ill injuries and just casually mentioned the good looking guy with the bandages on the top of his head that she just saw going down the hall on a stretcher. "Poor Guy", she said, I was in the Emergency Room when he was bought in and I wondered who he was" The floor nurse in charge replied quickly and said, Yes, he's been the talk of the floor because some woman hit him over the head with a beer bottle at the Pussy Cat Galore Strip Club the other night. Can you imagine?" Tina just laughed as she pursued her further for more information about him. Tina asked her where they were taking him and the floor nurse told her that Mr. Zodar was going down for his third scan of his brain because he has fluid building up and they may be doing surgery very soon. Bingo, Tina got exactly what she wanted information wise and now all she needed to do was check the shift duty roster to find out which room Mr. Toby Zodar was assigned to. Damn that girl has more going for her than any of us gave her credit for, such a good actress to boot!

Tina met us at the hospitality room in the basement of the hospital and had information that we never expected to hear. She said she observed Jake and Art, whom she recognized from that night hanging out in the family waiting area. They were all alone. Why weren't there family members in the waiting room and where was the other two men in their group? We couldn't hang out for long for fear of getting recognized. We decided to head back to the entrance of the hospital and watch from our vehicle when they leave the hospital and follow them. Tina stayed behind to let us know when these guys were on the way out of the hospital. Jan was not feeling too good from the lack of sleep and not eating properly so she just wanted to lay her head down somewhere. We now only have one more day left to find that damn video and as Jan crawls in the back of the Tahoe to lay down she says "I don't know how much more of this bullshit I can take. I really need to get home to my family". Little does she know we are about to encounter the worse of this nightmare.

Suddenly, as we were standing outside the vehicle, Judy says, "Oh My God, Get down". A black Mercedes with very dark tinted windows pulls up and out of it gets the fifth guy in the group that we recognize but don't know his name. Right behind him a woman with a scarf around her head and face steps out of the car. Judy and I are just beside ourselves now wondering who she is because we can't see much of her face and hair. We watched as they go through the entrance of the hospital and disappear. Then we both remembered at the same time that Tina's in there on watch and we need to warn her. Judy text her and Tina doesn't respond. I repeated by texting from my phone and again she doesn't respond. My heart is beating so fast I'm not sure

I will be able to catch my breath and Judy hurriedly wakes Jan up and tells her we have to go find Tina and for her to stay in the car with the engine running and pull up to the entrance just a few yards from the door. She gave Jan her cell phone because she didn't have hers anymore and told her we would stay in touch with mine. Looks like things are escalating sooner than we expected and we need to get the hell away now or something terrible is about to happen.

Judy and I enter the hospital from the Emergency Room side because we didn't want to be recognized. We head for the spot close to the waiting area where we left Tina, behind a group of tall green plants surrounding a rock fireplace on one side and a water fountain on the other side. She wasn't there. We stayed for a few minutes watching the now group of three guys and the suspicious looking woman. I told Judy I was going to the restroom to see if maybe Tina was there. When I returned without Tina, Judy's face was as white as if she had seen a ghost. "Look" she said. Coming down the hall way was Tina pushing a wheelchair with Toby in it and behind them was Jake, Art, Tim and the suspicious looking woman. They were heading for the exit and Jan was sitting outside in the car not far from it. We called her and told her to get out of there and park in the East parking lot adjacent to the entrance where she couldn't be seen. We explained we would find her and for her to be ready to follow the Mercedes. Now all we could do was observe what was about to happen next.

CHAPTER 11

Tina

WONDERING WHAT IS GOING on with Tina and why Toby was being released when Tina told us he was going to end up having surgery was so puzzling to Judy and I. "What the hell is going on", said Jan when we came running and jumped in the car. "Just follow that Mercedes because Tina is in it with Toby." At this point we were just clueless as to what was going on. Tina had acted so innocent but now we were suspicious that maybe somehow she had something to do with these gangsters. If that is true, we all were in some serious trouble. How could someone so damn quiet and shy turn out to be a part of whatever we are about to discover.

We followed the car to a warehouse off the interstate about ten miles down the road. It looked like it was a storage warehouse of some kind. Jan was afraid to stay too close so we pulled over in a piece of woods off the service road that led to it where we could at least watch from a distance. Thank God we found a set of binoculars in the vehicle so we were set to stake out every movement they made. I'm cringing because my phone has been ringing off the hook from my husband who thinks I will be home soon. I'm trying so hard to be cool about all of this because after all I was the one who wanted to make this damn trip to begin with. Jan is a nervous wreck because she and Tina had been so close to each other and she just can't see Tina being a part of any type of corruption. Regardless, here the three of us are now involved in something that we may never get out of and if it turns out that Tina is not a part of it, we all realize the danger we are about to face.

We can't involve the police and we can't get anywhere close to the building because some goon is walking around with a gun like he's some kind of security officer. It's decided that we would wait until dark, which would be in about an hour, before we make any kind of a move towards the warehouse. In the meantime, Judy is looking through Tina's purse that she left in the car when she went into the hospital. What she finds is about to send us through the roof! Not only did she have her fake ID that Judy had made for us to make this trip, she had a fake passport that shows her face and her nationality of Russian Federation. The passport date was December 11, 2012 and it was good for 10 years. "WTF" says Judy. As she digs deeper she finds a compartment in this huge purse that has a hidden pouch inside. Inside the pouch was a compact-loaded pistol that was made in Russia. My eyes were about to pop out of my head as Judy held it up and said, "OMG! Could Tina be a spy?" Jan says, " I think we should involve the police now." Judy and I both said at the same time, "No, we need to have more information about what we are talking about before we set foot inside a Police Department. After all we are all on the "Be on the lookout list", ourselves!

None of us seem to be able to figure this out because Tina, as we have said before, gave the impression of a shy and quiet non-violent person. I guess it's hard to judge a book by its cover.

We are still going to make a move on the building to at least see if we can see into it or hear something that will give us some clue as to what is happening inside.

Being on a stake out of this kind was all new to us but we are here and now is the time to make a move. "Now or never" says Jan. We decided that all three of us had to stick together no matter what was about to happen. If we had to fight, well so be it. After all that's what got us in the mess. Here we are slowly making our way through some pine thickets and marshy like land but with our adrenalin pumping we hardly noticed that we were walking through a damn swamp. Jan has the pistol with her and Judy is carrying the tire iron. As for myself, I had a compact flash light that put out just enough for us to see but we had to be careful not to shine it up in the air. I was so nervous I thought I was going to wet my pants. How could we be so damn bold and daring at this stage in our lives. Just as we thought we were close enough, all of a sudden, we see car lights coming up the service road. "Get down", Judy said. So as we fell to our knees in this stinking ass swamp we watched to see what was happening next. They pulled up in a big black Lincoln that shined like a diamond in the light from the moon. It was a very bright night and that was good for us because we tried to keep the flash light off as much as we could. As the car approached the warehouse we hear a horn blow and a big service door opens up and then closes. "That's just great", I said, " now we have more to worry about, we don't have a clue who is in that vehicle".

"Be quiet" says Jan, "did you all hear that", and about that time we hear a scream that sounds like its coming from a woman. Was it Tina, because it sure as hell sounded like her? Judy takes off running, as if she's Bat Woman and we had no choice but to chase behind her . We damn sure weren't going to let her charge in that place. We caught up to her when she was kneelin down beside an old beat up, broken down truck from the 1940's. We heard a scream again and by then we were sure it was not Tina. I'm frantic for whoever it was and was sure as hell not going to let it go so I decided to sneak around the back of this warehouse when the guard went the other direction. I told Judy and Jan to follow me one at a time after the guard comes back and turned around to head in the other direction. It was so dark I couldn't see a damn thing so I held onto the side of the building and very quietly and slowly moved around to the very back of it. Suddenly I felt a hand touch me and I freaked, then it went around my mouth. It was Judy and she knew I would scream but because we could only feel our way she knew she would have to keep me from making a noise. Then comes Jan and she's whispering that she was behind us. Ok so now what, I'm thinking to myself. We were near the part of the building where we could hear the voices in the building but the language was not understandable and then we heard Tina translating what someone was saying. Then it all starts to click. Tina worked as a translator for an Ambassador at the Pentagon when she was younger. It was still unclear though what the connection was with these guys. How could she do this to us, she knows everything about us and now we are caught up in what could turn out to be our worst nightmare.

CHAPTER 12

Captured

J AN WAS NOW HOLDING the pistol in her hand and really starting to get very anxious about this whole situation. She wanted to find out what was going on inside that warehouse so bad she could taste it. On the other hand, Pm sweating like I'm going to faint and Judy is not being the big bad ass redneck she was at the bar that night this all got started. Funny how things can change in a split second.

It wasn't five minutes before we hear another scream and heard Tina's voice again translating something. Jan moved a little further around the other side of the building and that's when we discovered there was a side door. Judy and I are trying to convince her that we are not the Charlie's Angels and that maybe it's time for us to get the hell out of there. Just about that time the door comes open and here we are standing there exposed to this frightening sight of a man who looked just like a Terrorist. Before Jan could blink an eye he grabbed her and took the pistol from her so fast she was in a state of shock. Judy and I took off running but we didn't get far because we ran right into the arms of two other horrid looking men who quickly had us under their control. Now we really are in the hands of the devil and have no clue what our destiny is going to be. We are being dragged by our hair into the building where another unfamiliar face does not appeal to us. Suddenly a cloth bag is put over our heads and we can no longer see anyone and the silence was so intense I'm shaking and praying that this was a dream and we would all wake up laughing, but that was as far from the truth as we could ever have been. Our lives were about to change forever and in the most ungodly forsaken way!

CHAPTER 13

Tortured

NOW WE ARE CAUGHT up in a more serious position than we could imagine and it was then that two women were speaking to each other in a foreign language and I recognized their voices. It was Mayla and Nata themselves. I knew we were dealing with people of a Russian descent. I felt someone touching me and running their hands up and down my clothing and I assumed it was to see if I had a weapon. Judy was mumbling something and I heard Tina say for her to keep her mouth shut. I never heard a word out of Jan and frankly I was totally petrified about this intensely dangerous situation and was praying that we would be able to convince these jerks to let us go home and forget what had taken place all together.

It seemed like hours before we were taken from where we were in the warehouse to another location somewhere in the building. I always had a great sense of smell and I noticed an aroma that was familiar to me. Oh my dear God in heaven what was going to happen. Suddenly I heard Jan screaming "no, no, no "and crying and begging "please don't". I spoke up immediately and said "what are you doing? Leave her alone"! That was the last thing I remember until I woke up, with the hooded cloth off my head, stripped of my clothing and tied to a bed post with my arms and legs spread eagle. As I moved my head I could see camera crews and bright lights and the room was decorated just like at the strip club. For some reason I couldn't talk, scream or mumble any sounds. My vision was blurred to the point I couldn't make out who the people were but I did recognize Tina being behind one of the video cameras. I knew I was involved now in a video and I wasn't liking what was happening to me. A door opens and in comes who I think is Judy and Jan with no hooded cloths on their heads but it was so many bright lights in my face I wasn't sure until I recognized Jan crying very deeply. I was drugged to the point I was very numb and still unable to speak. Suddenly, three men walked in to the room and disrobed. Two of them grabbed Jan and Judy and through their naked bodies on the bed. A third man, whom I recognized his voice to be Toby's, was on top of me and ordering the other two men to perform their parts in this movie while a group of what appeared to be soldiers were cheering them on while they raped each one of us numerous times. I was trying to scream and cry but there were no sounds coming from me. Toby was performing as if he was the main actor and started beating me with a huge black leather whip and telling me I was his forever and I would do whatever he commanded me to do. You are the one I wanted from the time I saw you walk through the door of the Pussy Cat Galore Club and now you will be my sex slave forever. He injected a needle in my arm and whispered in my ear that he would release me from being tied to the bed and I would perform to his favorite music and entertain the entire group of men using my body in any way he commanded me too. I listened as he told me to get on my knees and with that position I was forced to have oral sex with the two other me who had raped Judy and Jan, while Toby performed sex on me with a huge vibrator made of metal with large studs on it. I remember doing exactly as he told and felt like my body was being tortured to death. I just knew I was going to die and never see my family again but I had no control over things that were being done to me. I don't know what happened to Judy and Jan but these Russian men were torturous, cruel and women were their sex slaves. Mayla and Nata were Russian strippers brought to America to entertain and strip for men and women and they were also members of the Russian Militia. Tina was all a part of this from the beginning. She lived this secret life and we knew nothing about it until now. How could she be so involved in this type of sexual behavior and we not have a clue. Toby was the ring leader and the other guys were all actors who played the part of golfers to seduce women like ourselves.

Days later, I woke up in what they called the Russian Militia Underground and having no idea where I was until Toby informed me that I would never see my family again. He changed my named to Anna Bella and my entire identity. I was being trained for what Mayla and Nata were so good at doing and would be sent away never again to be returned to the United States. No one ever gets away from Toby and I so often wondered how my family was handling my disappearance and if in fact they would, by some miracle, find me.

My heart aches for my husband, children and family and as time goes by I become more and more mindful of how life use to be and how it is now. To this day I haven't a clue about my friends, Judy and Jan's, whereabouts or if they are even alive. Tina, on the other hand, is very active in the Militia and is known for her great pornography with this group of Russians.

These monsters are very sick bastards and find it amusing to carry out the destruction of many American women. I pray that someday I can find a way to flee from this horrible tortuous life and go home to my family, but most of the time I am kept so drugged that I hardly remember from day to day what is happening around me, I'm a sex slave to the leader of this Militia and he has vowed that I will never be released! Am I to be the next Naughty Nata of the Russian Underground?

www.ingramcontent.com/pod-product-compliance
Lightning Source LLC
Chambersburg PA
CBHW050429110726
47899CB00008B/2904